K

and the

Freaky Frog
Freakout

Peter H. Reynolds

WALKER
BOOKS

for Mary Lee
M. M.

to the Landry family
P. H. R.

First published 2013 by Walker Books Ltd
87 Vauxhall Walk, London SE11 5HJ

2 4 6 8 10 9 7 5 3 1

Text © 2013 Megan McDonald
Illustrations © 2013 Peter H. Reynolds

Stink ™. Stink is a registered trademark of
Candlewick Press, Inc, Somerville MA

This book has been typeset in Stone Informal

Printed in Great Britain by Clays Ltd, St Ives plc

British Library Cataloguing in Publication Data:
a catalogue record for this book is available from the British Library

ISBN 978-1-4063-4497-4

www.stinkmoody.com
www.walker.co.uk

CONTENTS

Croak!

Squeenk!

Ribbet!

The shark was super sneaky. The shark was super slithery. The shark slid through the water like a silver streak.

Stink felt something grab his leg. S-s-shark attack!

"AARGH!" Stink leaped out of the way, making a big, giant ker-splash!

The sneaky shark was … his sister, Judy!

"Hey! No sneaking up on me like that in the pool. You scared my pants off!"

"That's because I'm a Shark and you're a Polliwog. You're going to have to put your head underwater some time, Stink. You can't stay a Polliwog for ever. I'm almost a Barracuda!"

Sometimes, Stink wished he didn't have to take swimming lessons with Judy-the-almost-Barracuda. She was always bugging him to hold his breath and put his head underwater.

No, thanks. He'd tried that once already when a kid named Dunk had dunked him. OK, so Dunk wasn't his *real* name. But Stink still got a Major Nose Wedgie! Why would he want a geyser up his nose *on purpose*?

Riley Rottenberger was the one and only second-grade Shark. And Webster and Sophie were already Dolphins.

"I know how to swim," Stink told Judy.

"If you call doggie-paddling swimming," said Judy.

"I can swim across the pool," said Stink.

"Without a pool noodle?" Judy asked. Stink's shoulders sagged.

"C'mon," said Judy. "Just hold your breath and stick your face in the water."

"Hello! Nose wedgie!" said Stink. Nose wedgies were scary. And they burned. And made you choke. Stink had been breathing air for over seven years and he was fine with that.

"Sharks get to dive for quarters," said Judy.

Dive for quarters! Stink wanted to dive for quarters! But that meant holding his breath all the way to the bottom of the pool. He shivered. "Maybe next week."

"Stink!" called Cammy, his swim teacher. "Lesson's over. Time to go."

"See? Time to go," said Stink.

"Have it your way," said Judy. "But I'm going to dive for quarters one last time. Not pennies. Not nickels. Not dimes, Stink. Quarters." She grinned like a sawtooth barracuda, then swam off silvery-smooth like a shark.

Stink clung to his pool noodle in the shallow end, watching the Sharks dip and dive and come up for air.

Polliwog-a-doodle-all the day.

∗ ∗ ∗

Then something unusual happened! Stink climbed up out of the pool. He flip-flopped his way into the boys' locker room. He flicked on the shower, turning his back to the hot water.

That's when he saw it. Something lumpy and bumpy in the corner of the shower. Something bigger than a spider. Something greener than a spider.

Stink turned off the shower and bent down to get a closer look. *SPROING!* The bumpy lump jumped!

"It's alive!" Stink yelled.

Ribbet! Ribbet-ribbet! The bumpy

lump was a frog! A teeny-weeny greeny frog.

"What are you doing in here, little guy?" Stink asked. "You're far away from home, aren't you?"

Wait just a frog-hoppin' minute! Something was not right. Something was way wrong with that frog.

That frog had only one-two-three-not-four legs!

"Did you almost get eaten?" Stink asked. "Some big bad bird ate a frog leg for dinner, didn't he?"

Stink knew he *had* to rescue the frog. He bent down and cupped his hands over the little guy. "Gotcha!"

Sproing! The little green three-legged froggy leapfrogged right out of Stink's hands.

Stink tried again. He cupped his hands. He waited, waited, waited and pounced. "Gotcha!"

Sproing! That froggy leaped right out of Stink's hands again.

Stink chased that froggy in circles around the shower.

Sproing! The frog leaped onto the drain cover. *Sproing!* The frog leaped up on the wall. *Sproing!* The frog leap-frogged right inside Stink's swimming goggles.

Pounce! "Mine at last," said Stink.

* * *

Stink showed the frog to Judy. Stink showed the frog to Webster and Sophie of the Elves. Stink showed the frog to Riley Rottenberger.

"Meet King Otto," said Stink. "King of the three-legged frogs."

"More like Frogzilla!" said Riley. Everybody cracked up.

"So cute," said Judy.

"So tiny," said Sophie.

"So green," said Webster.

"So many warts," said Riley.

Stink peeked at the frog again. He was bright shiny green with black eyes and a white racing stripe down his side.

"Those aren't warts, those are—"

"Beauty marks," Sophie teased. "Ooh-la-la."

"I was going to say freckles," said Stink.

Everybody leaned in closer to peer at Stink's frog.

"Too bad about his leg," said Judy.

"Still, he'll make the perfect friend for Toady," said Stink.

"Yeah, if your toad wants a freak of nature for a friend," said Riley.

"You can't keep him," said Judy.

"You can't keep him," said Webster and Sophie.

"You can't keep him," said Riley Rottenberger.

"We'll see," said Stink.

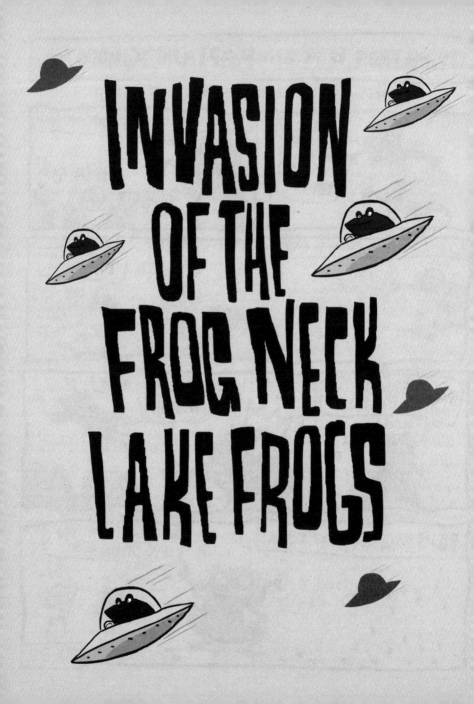

Stink took one giant leap for frog kind. He let King Otto go in the Great Outdoors.

But when he got home, the strangest thing happened. Stink had his air-breathing nose in Amazing Spider-Man comic book issue #159: *Arm-in-Arm-in-Arm-in-Arm-in-Arm-in-Arm with Doctor Octopus.* Stink went down the steps. *OK, I'll work with you, Octopus – but I won't shake your hand!* Stink walked to the front door. *We get a move on, Doc – and fast! Or it's Swiss Cheese City for both of us!* Stink started to slip on his boots.

Cra-awk! A little green frog leaped out of his boot, hopped down the steps and sprang into the grass.

Stink dropped the Amazing Spider-Man #159. He sprang after the frog. "At least you have all your legs," said Stink. Sock-footed, he chased it through grass and mud on all fours. But the little four-footer blended into the grass. He was so fast on his little frog feet, he got away.

"I give up," said Stink. He went to squirt off his muddy hands, but no water came out of the hose.

"Great," said Stink. He picked up his comic book and raced inside. He wipe-wipe-wiped the bottoms of his socks. They were still muddy. And grassy.

That's the end of you, Hammerhead. Stink peeled off his socks and tiptoed upstairs to the bathroom. *Being a superhero is no bed of roses.* Stink turned on the water in the tub to rinse his feet.

Sproing! Something caught his eye. Not a rubber ducky. Not a floaty boaty. A froggy woggy! A real live blinking frog!

Stink could not believe his eyes.

He had heard of it raining cats and dogs. But whoever heard of it raining frogs! He cast about, looking for something he could use to catch the frog.

"Don't-go-away-don't-go-away,"

Stink urged in a soft voice. Keeping one eye on the frog, he grabbed a cup and *slammo!* He scooped up the little tree frog and raced downstairs.

"Me! Frog! Found! Tree! Three!" Stink ran out onto the back deck, wild-eyed and out of breath.

"Stink, honey," said Mum. "Slow down."

"You sound like an alien," said Judy.

"What are you trying to tell us?" asked Dad.

"It's raining frogs!" said Stink. "Not cats. Not dogs. Frogs. I found three green tree frogs today. One at the pool, one in my boot and one in the tub. Just now."

Stink lifted his hand to show the little green frog in the cup.

"In the tub? I did notice that a frog keeps hopping out of the garden hose when I go to water the roses," said Mum.

"They're in the garage too," said Dad. "And I'm sure I heard one in the basement."

"Maybe it's all this rain we've been having," said Mum.

"Maybe it's the first sign of spring," said Dad.

"Maybe Stink is like a big giant human frog magnet," said Judy. "And all the frogs come out when he's around."

"I bet they know I'm a friend to all amphibians," said Stink. "I mean, I have a pet toad, and I had a pet newt, even though Judy let him go down the drain—"

"I didn't *let* him," Judy protested.

"And I read everything there is to know about skinks in the *S* encyclopedia. That counts. And I like the gecko ad on TV." He leapfrogged around the deck and all the way across the yard to the back fence.

When he got to the creek, he let the frog go in the Pond of Life.

"Avoid big bad birds," Stink told the little frog. "And may you live froggily every after."

* * *

Sunday and Monday were no-frog days. Not even a toad. Tuesday too. On Wednesday, Stink saw five more frogs crossing the road on the way home from swimming. On Thursday, Stink saw a picture of a giant half-metre-long Goliath frog in his *Geo Kids* magazine. It was almost half as tall as Stink! No lie. On Friday, Stink could hardly sleep, the frogs outside were so loud. He had to count frogs-not-sheep to go to sleep.

Then came Saturday. Swimming lessons again. Stink got wet up to his neck. He even dunked his left ear in the water. And he won a crab race across the pool (without putting his head under).

After swimming class, Stink talked Sophie and Webster into going on a nature walk.

"Nature walk," said Riley Rottenberger. "You don't get to see anything on those walks except nature."

"That's what we want to see!" said Sophie.

"No, I mean, it's just trees and plants and dead leaves. Not even poison ivy."

"Um, hello! Nobody wants to nature walk through poison ivy," said Stink.

"Maybe we'll see a flying squirrel," said Sophie.

"Or a bobcat," said Webster.

"You guys! Trust me. There are no animals."

"Not even animal tracks?" asked Webster.

"Not even animal droppings?" asked Sophie.

"Not unless you count mosquitoes,"

said Riley. "I got about two hundred mosquito bites when I had to go on a nature walk. And a gnat went up my nose."

"Don't worry, you guys," said Stink. "This is different. It's not even in the woods."

"It's not?" asked Sophie.

"It's not?" asked Webster.

"No," said Stink. "It's at a pool."

"But we're already at the pool," said Webster.

"The kind of pool that has frogs and lizards and salamanders and turtles."

"And dead leaves," said Riley.

"Coolness," said Sophie.

"Coolness," said Webster.

"Have fun counting mosquito bites," said Riley. She waved goodbye.

Riley Rottenberger was a real sour ball sometimes.

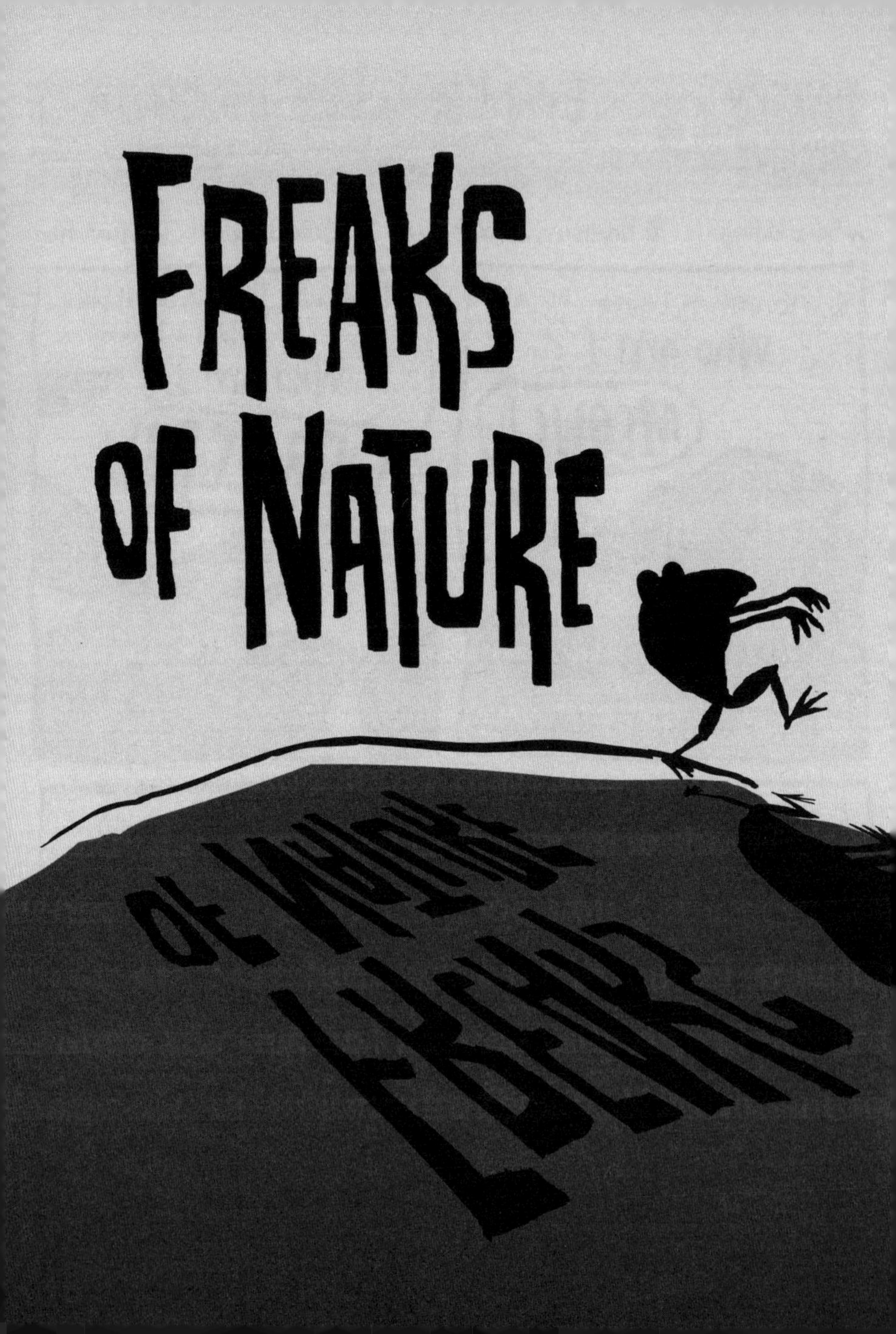
FREAKS
OF NATURE

Later that afternoon, when Dad, Stink and his friends got to the nature centre, a young guy came out to meet them.

"Hi, I'm Jasper," said the guy. He was tall and had a tiny beard on his chin. He wore a hat with a wide brim, a vest covered with little pockets and wellie boots up to his knees.

Dad shook hands with him and the kids all told him their names.

"I'm a grad student at the local college," said Jasper. "And I'll be your guide. Looks like it's just us today, huh? Everybody grab a bucket and a net. Let's head over to the vernal pool."

The vernal pool was a small wetland surrounded by trees. Pussy willows and bulrushes lined the banks.

"Are there bobcats here?" asked Webster.

"Are there flying squirrels here?" Sophie asked.

"You guys!" said Stink.

"How about mosquitoes?" Sophie scratched an imaginary mosquito bite.

"Mostly amphibians," said Jasper. "Luckily they eat all the mosquitoes."

"Amphibians are my favourite!" said Stink. "Especially frogs. Also skinks. And newts. I even make up comics about this superhero called Stink Frog."

"Sounds cool. What does he do?"

"Mostly he fights slime. But he's really good at swimming and he can put his head all the way under and he can jump higher than the Empire State Building. And once he saved the earth from a giant spitball. You know, like Spider-Man and the asteroid."

"So, you're into Spider-Man?" said Jasper. "I used to collect Spider-Man comics."

"Really? My dad did too. I'm reading some of his from the seventies!"

Dad nodded. "Stink, let's give Jasper a chance to tell us about the pond."

"This is a vernal pool," said Jasper. "That means it's a wetland that's here mostly from rain and melted snow. Vernal pools are great habitats for all kinds of frogs, toads, turtles and salamanders."

"I have a Stuffed Animal Baby named Salamandra," Sophie chimed

43

in. "Made of crushed orange velvet."

They walked out onto a short wooden dock that jutted out over the pond. "Shh!" said Jasper. He pointed. Five painted turtles sunned themselves on a rock. A small blue-tailed skink darted across the dock. Two red dragonflies dipped and dived over the pond. Water striders skipped across the surface.

"Is that a stick bug?" asked Stink, pointing to a bug that looked like a stick.

"A *stink*bug?" said Webster, holding his nose closed.

"That's a water scorpion," said Jasper. He took them down to the banks of the pond and lifted up some leaf litter. Curled up underneath was a black salamander with yellow spots.

"Spotted salamander?" Dad asked.

"Yep. They're making a comeback," said Jasper.

Jasper let everybody dip nets and buckets in the water. "Dip your bucket in, take a look and then put it back," said Jasper.

Sophie caught a fairy shrimp in her bucket. Webster caught a diving beetle. And Stink caught … a stick.

A stick with glup on it. "Hey! There's a polka-dot jellyfish on my stick," said Stink, pointing to a clear jelly-like glob on the stick.

"Looks like it could be an egg mass of the spotted salamander," said Jasper. "Hopefully each one of those polka

dots will hatch into a salamander."
He carefully set the stick back in the
water.

They walked all the way around to
the other side of the pool.

"I think I hear a frog!" said Stink.

"You should hear it just after dark,"
said Jasper. "It's like a frog party out
here. I know technically it's still winter,
but in the heart of a frog, it's spring."
He reached down and scooped up a
brown leaf.

The brown leaf was a frog!

"This is a wood frog," said Jasper.
"It's more brown than other frogs, and

it has a dark mask behind each eye. They sound like, *Craw-awk, craw-awk!* We catch them and study them and it teaches us stuff about the frogs."

"*Craw-awk!*" Stink croaked. "*Craw-awk!*"

"Frogs have been popping up all over the place at our house lately," said Dad.

"We've been getting calls about that," said Jasper. "Frogs are popping up all over town. Their habitats are shrinking from so much building going on in our area. And with climate changes, there aren't as many wetlands and vernal pools, so frogs seek out water wherever they can find it."

"Stink found a frog in the shower at the pool!" said Sophie.

"And it only had three legs!" said Stink.

"I'm sorry to hear that," said Jasper. "Unfortunately, we're finding more and more frogs that have something wrong with them." He shook his head. "It's not a good sign."

"Really?" asked Stink. "I thought his leg just got eaten by a big bad bird."

"I'm afraid not. All kinds of weird

things happen to frogs because of fertilizer, pesticides and pollution in the water. C'mon back to the centre and I'll show you."

At the nature centre, Jasper showed them not-normal frogs in tanks. One frog had an extra leg and one had what looked like a crooked tail. Stink picked up one that had three eyes.

"Freaky-deaky!" said Stink. "Does this one have a name?"

"Not that I know of," said Jasper.

"I dub you King Otto the Second," said Stink. Jasper laughed.

"Weird," said Webster. "You can see

Three Legs   Crooked Tail

through that one. Casper the Friendly Ghost Frog."

"Casper the *Freaky* Ghost Frog," said Sophie. Webster cracked up.

"These frogs have a hard time making it in the wild," said Jasper. "They'd probably just get eaten."

Three eyes   See Through

"Oosh. Being a frog is no bed of roses," Stink said.

"You sound like Spider-Man!" Jasper said.

Stink grinned.

"So that's why we rescue any abnormal frogs and study them. Here at the centre, we have all kinds of initiatives to save the frogs."

"That's great. Isn't it, Stink?" Dad said. Stink nodded.

"You know, if you're really into frogs, you should come to the First Annual Frog Neck Lake Frog Count next Friday night. It's perfect weather for counting frogs."

"Really?" Stink asked.

"Sure! We're concerned that the number of frogs in our area is down, so a bunch of us are meeting up at Frog Neck Lake to count frogs at night."

"A frog stakeout!" said Stink. "Do

you stay up late and drink coffee and stuff?"

"Sure. Hot chocolate too."

"But how do you see the frogs at night?" Webster asked.

"You don't see them. You *hear* them. You learn to identify each frog by its call. Then you count which ones you hear."

"Sounds interesting," said Dad.

"Can we come too?" asked Webster.

"The more the merrier. We need all the help we can get. But one of you will have to learn some frog calls. I can show you a website that has all the frog sounds. Also, you have to pass a quiz before I can sign you up."

"Quiz? I love tests," said Stink.

"It's true. He really does," Dad said, nodding.

"What do frogs do with a Maths test?" Stink asked.

"I don't know. What?" said Jasper.

"They Rip-it! Rip-it!" said Stink. Stink cracked himself up.

Pree-eep! Craw-awk! Sque-enk!

Stink listened to frog calls on the computer. He listened to frog sounds that he recorded with his own digital recorder (by sticking it out the window at night!). Stink listened to frog calls on the way to school on Monday morning and in the car on the way to swimming lessons.

Pre-eep! Craw-awk! Sque-enk! At swimming, he tried some out on his friends.

"You sound like a duck," said Webster.

"You sound like a squeaky toy," said Sophie.

"You sound like a sick banjo," said Riley.

"Thanks!" said Stink. "See, spring peepers sound like squeaky toys. And wood frogs sound like ducks quacking."

"You're quacked," said Webster. Sophie and Riley cracked up.

"You guys sound like Southern

leopard frogs. A leopard frog sounds like a person laughing. No lie."

"Yeah, but nothing sounds like a sick banjo," said Riley.

"Nothing except for the Northern green frog. It sounds like a loose banjo string. You know, like a rubber-band twang."

"You sure are freaky for frogs," said Riley.

"Thanks!" said Stink.

"You should marry a frog, you like them so much."

"Hardee-har-har," said Stink.

* * *

Stink could not wait till swimming was over. He had a freaking great idea for how to learn frog sounds. He would need a comb, a balloon, two rocks, a can of spray paint, a rubber band, a rubber duck, some jingle bells and that's all.

Stink blew up the balloon and rubbed it with his hand. He clicked rocks together. He twanged a rubber band.

Judy poked her head into Stink's room. Mouse squeezed past her. "Stink, I'm trying to study my times tables and I can't hear myself—" She stopped when she saw the pile of junk on Stink's floor.

"What? I'm using this stuff to make frog sounds. Here, I'll show you." Stink rubbed his finger along the teeth of a comb. "This sounds like a chorus frog." Stink shook the can of spray paint.

"And this sounds like a Northern cricket frog."

Mouse darted under the bed.

"And this – *AARGH!* – sounds like Mum when she sees the mess in your room," said Judy.

"Hardee-har-har," chuckled Stink. "You're *croaking* me up!"

"Can you please shut your door so I don't have to hear Froggle Rock all day?"

* * *

Stink squeaked his rubber duck down the stairs. He snored up a storm while he made a snack. He shook the can of paint, clicked the stones and jingled the bells. "Wood frog, pickerel frog, cricket frog," he recited.

"Stink, keep it down, please," said Dad, poking his head around the corner. "I'm on the phone."

"No spray-painting in the house," said Mum. "Take that outside."

"I'm not painting," said Stink. "Doesn't anybody around here know a Northern cricket frog when they hear one?"

Mum crinkled her forehead.

"It's homework," said Stink. "I have to take a test."

"A *frog* test," said Judy, coming into the kitchen.

"I have to learn frog calls," said Stink. "For the First Annual Frog Neck Lake Frog Count on Friday."

"Riigggght," said Mum.

"It's a real thing. The test is on the computer," Stink told her. "You click on a frog and it makes a sound. Then you guess which frog is making that sound."

"Multiple choice?" said Judy. "Easy peasy," she teased.

"I have a multiple choice for you," said Mum. "You can go back upstairs

and a) finish your homework, b) finish your homework, c) finish your home-work, or d) all of the above."

"But—" Stink protested.

"It's your choice," Mum said.

Stink trudged back up the stairs, with Judy close behind.

"And don't forget your NON-frog homework too," Mum called.

✳   ✳   ✳

In Stink's room, Mouse was curled up on his backpack. "How am I going to learn all these frog calls by Tuesday?" Stink asked Judy. He held out his note-book for her to see. "You can't go on the frog count unless you pass the quiz. Jasper said."

"I'll help you," said Judy. "But let's make it a game. Instead of Rock, Paper, Scissors, we'll call it ... Rock, Balloon, Squeaky Toy."

"How do we play?"

"Close your eyes. I'll make a sound. You guess which frog it is. But we have to keep it down because Mum won't like us doing *frog* homework first."

"OK, c'mon," said Stink. He squeezed his eyes shut. Judy rubbed the balloon. She twanged the rubber band. She clicked the stones.

"Mrrow!" Mouse pawed at the stones.

"Chorus frog. Wood frog. Cricket frog," Stink guessed.

Judy checked Stink's notebook. "Sorry. Leopard frog. Green frog. Cricket frog."

Stink hung his head.

"Hey, you got one right. Cricket frog. C'mon, Stink. Just get super-duper quiet. And really listen. OK. Ready?"

"Ready, Freddy," said Stink.

Judy rubbed, clicked, squeaked and twanged.

"Balloon, stones, squeaky toy, rubber band," Stink said. "That's leopard

71

frog, cricket frog, spring peeper, green frog."

"Bingo!" said Judy. She laughed, chuckled, whistled, peeped, snored, squeaked, jingled and croaked until Stink knew pickerel frog from peeper, chorus frog from cricket.

"Yikes," said Judy, putting a *shh*-finger to her lips. "I bet they can hear us all the way at the end of Croaker Road."

"Do you think they call our street Croaker Road because of all the frogs?"

"Because of animal frogs, Stink, not human boy frogs."

"Ribbet!" Stink croaked.

"OK, close your eyes. I bet I can stump you. Ready?" Judy made a *zzzzz* sound.

"Bullfrog. No. Wood frog. No. Bullfrog." He opened his eyes.

"Zipper frog," said Judy. "That was just me zipping the zipper on your backpack."

"No fair," said Stink. "There's no such thing as a zipper frog."

"Mrrr-ow!" Mouse pounced on the jingle bells.

"Jingle frog!" Stink and Judy said at the same time. They cracked themselves up.

"We have to finish our NOT-frog homework, Stink. Besides, you're like the Frog King now. No, you're like President of the Frogs. Now you just have to practise on real frogs."

"Sque-enk!" said Stink.

A. Southern leopard frog B. Northern green frog C. Northern spring peeper frog D. Wood frog

1. X marks the spot on my back. Who am I?

TWEE! TWEE! TWEE!

2. I'll eat anything — even dead, shed skin. YUM! Who am I?

SQUEENK!

3. Call me Bandit Frog. I have a robber mask like a raccoon. Who am I?

CRA-AAWK!

4. Night-time is my time. I'm puttin' on da ribbet! Who am I?

HA-HA-HA-HA-HA!

ANSWERS ON PAGE 158

On Tuesday, Stink Moody, Frog Genius, passed his test with flying colours. Frog test, that is.

Now if only he could pass a put-your-head-under-the-water swimming test too. On Wednesday, Stink got wet up-to-but-not-including his nose. He dipped his left *and* right ear in the water. He leaned way back and got his hair wet.

"Go, Stink," said Cammy, his swim-ming teacher. "Now let's see if you can blow bubbles." Stink blew bubbles with his mouth. He almost-just-about-not-quite blew bubbles with his nose.

Almost!

Someday, Stink would even get his eyeballs wet. He wished he had gills, like a tadpole. He wished he could breathe through his skin like a frog. *Ribbet!*

* * *

Stink could not wait for Frog Friday. At last, it was Friday night. Frog night. Time for the First Annual Frog Neck Lake Frog Count.

At three minutes before sunset, Stink loaded up his backpack. Torch. Back-up Torch. Pen. Thermometer. Timer. Digital recorder. At seven minutes after sunset, Stink called Frog Assistant Number One and Frog Assistant Number Two (aka Webster and Sophie of the Elves.)

"Meet me at the Frog Neck Lake car park. T-minus 27 minutes and counting."

When Dad dropped him off, Stink ran over to Sophie and Webster. The car park was humming with frog counters. There was a white-haired guy wearing a headlamp, a couple with matching T-shirts that said VIRGINIA IS FOR FROGS and a teenager with froggy wellies.

"People sure are freaky for frogs, huh?" said Webster.

Jasper waved Stink over. "Stink! Thanks for coming, dude. You guys are right on time. Hey, before I forget, I have something for you." He handed Stink a plastic bag with two comic books. "I had a couple extras. Thought you might like them."

"Amazing Spider-Man Comic Book Number 414: *From Darkness Strikes – Delilah!* Whoa! She's the one who brought Dr Octopus back to life."

"In the other one," said Jasper, "Spidey shrinks down to spider-size."

"Wow! Thanks!" Stink put them away in his backpack for safekeeping.

"And ... here's your official Frog Log," said Jasper.

"Frog Log. Cool beans!" said Stink.

Jasper showed Stink where to write down the time and the temperature. "And don't forget sky, rain and wind conditions."

Stink nodded.

"Listen up, everybody," said Jasper. "It's time to head out and spread out. Don't forget. Use your thermometers to record air temps. Set your timers to five minutes. Then record what species you hear on the ACI. That's the Amphibian Calling Index. Got it?"

Everybody nodded.

"Are you ready to ribbet?" asked Jasper.

✳ ✳ ✳

A light rain fell. The night air smelled like worms. *Cro-oak! Cra-awk!* The pond was a symphony of frogs.

Stink filled in his Frog Log. Time:

7:56 p.m. Temp: 55 degrees. Sky code: five, for light rain, drizzle. Stink licked his finger and held it in the air to check the wind. Wind code: two. Gentle breeze.

"Wow. There must be a million frogs out here," said Sophie.

"Yeah, maybe they're singing bed-time songs," said Stink. "Like a frog sleepover."

"They don't sound sleepy to me," said Webster. He put his fingers in his ears.

"Guys! The number one rule of frog counting is QUIET. Frogs will stop sing-ing if we make too much noise. When

84

I start the timer, we have to be quiet for five minutes."

"Five whole minutes?" asked Webster.

"Sophie, you hold the umbrella over me," said Stink.

"Why does she get to hold the umbrella?" asked Webster.

"Because ... she's Frog Assistant Number Two. But Frog Assistant Number One gets to ... hold the torch. So I can see what I'm writing."

Stink set the timer. He tilted his head, closed his eyes and listened. Peeper frogs peeped and chorus frogs preeped. Leopard frogs laughed and green frogs thrummed like they were playing the banjo. *C'tung! C'tung!*

Stink made a tick in his notebook for each kind of frog he heard.

"What do you hear?" Webster asked.

"I hear *you*," said Stink.

"I'm bored," said Webster.

"Wait. I hear a dog barking," said Stink. "Noise level: two."

"I hear a car on the road," said Sophie.

"Noise level: three. For car noise," said Stink.

"I hear a cat," said Webster.

"It's probably a bullfrog," said Stink.

"When a bullfrog is scared, it sounds like a cat."

"Now it sounds more like a cow. Is it true you can hear them, like, a mile away? And is it true that one bullfrog can eat a whole snake? And is it true—"

"Noise level: Six. For the talking assistant."

"Oops." Webster held his hand over his mouth. He aimed the torch up at the sky.

"Webster. The light. I can't see." Stink made a mark for a spring peeper.

"But I thought I saw a shooting star," said Webster. "My arm is tired."

"At least you're not holding the umbrella," said Sophie, switching hands. "My arm's about to fall off!"

"Shh!" said Webster. "I heard something." He trained the light on the woods behind them. Just then, all three friends heard a sound coming from the trees.

Snap!

"Bobcat!" Webster dared to whisper.

"Or a vampire flying frog!" Sophie whispered.

Snap! Snap! Twigs snapped. Leaves crunched underfoot.

"Maybe it's a moose," said Webster.

"There're no meese … I mean mice … I mean moose in Virginia," said Stink.

"Maybe it's a moose *frog*," said Webster.

"No such thing," said Stink.

Snap! Crunch! The not-moose was getting closer. Stink pricked up his ears. Closer, closer…

"Aagh!" All three kids screamed. Webster dropped the torch. Sophie's umbrella went flying.

"Hi, guys!" said Jasper.

"Jasper!" said Stink. "You scared our pants off!"

"We thought you were a moose," said Sophie.

"Or a moose *frog*," said Webster.

"Sorry. Didn't mean to sneak up on you. Just came over to see how it's going."

"Great!" said Stink. "So far I've heard six peeper frogs. One big fat bullfrog. And a load of others too. See?"

"Good job," said Jasper, shining a light on Stink's notebook. "Let me know if you hear any barking tree frogs. They're pretty much endangered now, but you never know. Thanks, guys."

As soon as Jasper left, Webster pulled up his hood and shifted from foot to foot. "I'm wet," said Webster.

"I'm cold," said Sophie.

"I'm hungry," said Stink.

The frogs went quiet. Not a peep.

"Let's count marshmallows," said Stink. "In our hot chocolate."

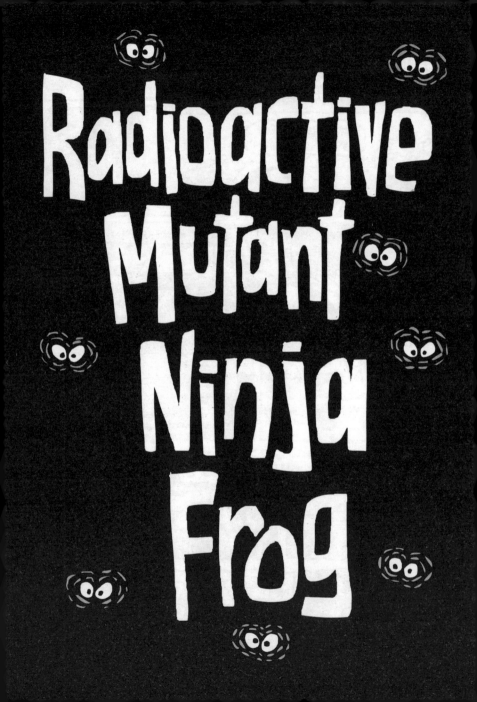

Radioactive Mutant Ninja Frog

The Slime rushed along the underground tunnel and oozed up through the manhole into the streets. Cars and cabs got smeared with slime. Buses and trains dripped with slime. Fire trucks and stop signs turned from red to green.

The whole city was one big mess. Streets crawled with sewer rats. Swimming pools oozed with green gunk. This was a job for Stink Frog.

He uncurled his mile-long tongue. But not even he could lick up all the—

"Aagh!" Stink swiped at his left arm, waking up from his dream, where he was swimming in ... cat slobber! "Mouse, stop licking. That tickles!"

RIBBET!

Stink opened one eye. It was not a cat licking his arm. It was not a dog. It was not a guinea pig. It was a...

"Frog!" yelled Stink. He bolted awake. "Hey! How did you get—"

The frog leaped. Stink glanced at the open backpack on his bed. The Spider-Man comic books spilled out of it.

Last night, Stink had been so tired, he did not have to count frogs-not-sheep to get to sleep. He fell asleep reading Amazing Spider-Man #414.

Stink scooped up the frog. "Hey? Did you get into my backpack last night at the lake or something?"

The frog blinked. Stink stared at the frog.

Wait just a frog-hopping minute! Something was not right. Something was wrong. Very, very wrong.

Stink rubbed his eyes. He shook his head. He pinched himself. Ouch! He was awake all right. This was no-way-no-how-NOT a dream.

The frog did not have three legs. The frog did not have five legs. The frog did not have an extra eye or a freaky tail.

The frog was *blue*.

Blue like the sky-blue crayon. Blue

like the sky-blue sky. Blue as in NOT green. No lie!

This frog was not normal. This frog was mutant. This frog was ninja. This frog was ... radioactive! *Was it? Could it be? No way. But it must be. How else do you explain a blue frog?*

And ... the frog had *licked* Stink. Just like the spider that bit Peter Parker!

Freaky frog freakout! A real-live radioactive mutant frog had licked him – right on the freckle on his left arm. Stink would never ever wash that spot again.

This was the best day ever! And it was only 8:31 a.m.

✱ ✱ ✱

At 8:45 a.m., Stink set up an old fish-bowl for the mutant frog – King Otto the Third. He hid it under his Spider-Man pyjama shirt. He hid that under his desk.

A blue frog! And this rarest of frogs, this radioactive mutant ninja frog, had licked *him*. Stink E. Moody.

This was a thing so secret, Stink did not tell anybody. He kept the freaky frog all to himself – for a little while.

He would wait. Wait for something unusual to happen.

Something Peter Parker-ish.

At 9:03 a.m., Stink went downstairs for breakfast. At 9:05, Stink ate a bowl of cereal. At 9:06, Stink said, "Is it just me? Or do these raisins look like dead flies?"

"You hate raisins," said Judy.

Glup! "Not anymore," said Stink.

"Here, you can have my dead flies too," said Judy. She plopped three wrinkly dead-fly raisins into his bowl.

"Stink. Milk. On your nose," said Mum, pointing to her own nose.

Slurp! At 9:13, Stink touched the tip of his nose with his tongue. *Holy cow! I didn't know I could do that,* thought Stink.

"Weird!" Judy wiggled her own tongue up towards her nose.

"Not even close," said Stink.

"Since when can you touch your nose with your tongue?"

"Since eight thirty-one this morning," he told Judy. *Since I got licked by a mutant frog!* He didn't dare say it out loud. *But wait ... was it true? For real?*

102

Stink stuck out his tongue and tried again. *It worked! Amazing!*

"Kids," said Mum. "Let's keep our tongues in our mouths at the table."

At 9:26, Stink put his bowl in the sink. He leapfrogged around the kitchen.

"Can I play outside?" he asked Mum.

"It's pouring with rain," said Judy. "You hate the rain."

"Nah-uh. I'm just going to splash in mud puddles," said Stink.

"Wear your boots!" Mum called.

At 9:43, Stink developed a new interest in mud. He also had a new fascination  with worms. *Shazam! He was getting froggier by the second!*

Stink went on a worm hunt. He held worm races.

He conducted the First Annual Great Backyard Earthworm Count.

He even wondered what it would be like to eat a squirmy worm.

Stink was building a worm tower when Mum called him inside.

"What were you doing out in the rain all that time?" asked Judy.

"Worm stuff," said Stink.

"You hate worms," said Judy.

"Not."

"Since when?" Judy asked. "And don't say eight thirty-one this morning."

"Actually, it was more like nine forty-three this morning," said Stink.

Judy looked at him strangely. She tilted her head sideways.

"Is it time for swimming yet?" Stink asked.

"No swimming lessons today, Stink."

"But it's Saturday!" said Stink.

"The pool's closed for— Hey, wait just a sneaky-shark second. You hate swimming."

"You're cuckoo," said Stink. "Never mind. I know something else I can do."

Stink raced upstairs. He put on his swimming fins. He put on his wet suit. He flop-flop-flopped down the stairs. He flop-flop-flopped into the kitchen. He flip-flopped over to the kitchen sink.

Stink filled the sink with water. He put on his swimming goggles. He stuck his face in the sink. He blew bubbles!

Stink put on his snorkel next and lowered his head to the water again.

Judy came into the kitchen. "What are you doing?"

"Blub, blub, blub," Stink gurgled.

"Mum!" Judy called. "Stink's swimming in the kitchen sink!"

Today, the sink. Tomorrow, the pool! There was no stopping him now.

Mum rushed into the kitchen. "Stink?" she asked. "What's going on here?"

"Practice. Swimming," Stink said around the mouthpiece. "I can't be a Polliwog for ever."

Mum put her hands on her hips. Mum looked like she didn't know what to say.

Dad came into the kitchen. "What's going on?" he asked.

"Can't anybody tell I'm swimming?" asked Stink.

"Stink's swimming in the sink!" said Judy.

"Any chance you can save swimming for the pool?" Dad asked. "I have to do the dishes now."

"Fine." Stink stopped swimming. He took off his snorkel. He took off his goggles. He let the water drain out of the sink. He poli-wiggled out of his wetsuit. He poli-woggled out of his swimming fins.

"Hey, Dad, can I sleep in the basement tonight?" Stink asked.

"It's too damp down there," said Dad.

"And cold," said Mom.

"And don't forget spiders," said Judy. "You hate spiders. And basements."

Stink did hate the basement. But that was before. "Stop saying I hate stuff."

"The facts, Stink." Judy ticked off on her fingers. "First raisins. Then rain. Then worms. Then swimming in the sink. Now you want to sleep in the creepy, cold basement? What's the matter with you?"

"None of your big-sister beeswax," said Stink. "It's a secret."

Peter Parker picked a peck of pickled peepers! Stink *was* turning into an F-R-O-G frog! For real! No lie. Even Judy saw it.

"Never mind. I'll sleep in my own bed," said Stink. "But I can still go swimming in the *upstairs* sink." He grabbed his wetsuit, snorkel, mask and fins.

Judy walked up the stairs backwards, giving Stink the stink eye.

"Spiders don't scare me, you know. I eat spiders for breakfast."

"Since when?" asked Judy.

"Since—" Stink stopped. *Should he say it? Out loud?*

"What's the matter? Got a *frog* in your throat?" Judy stopped on the top stair. "Wait a second." She squinted at Stink like she was seeing him for the very first time.

"Mum! Dad!" called Judy. "Stink thinks he's a frog!"

CREATURE FEATURE 3

FREAKY FROGS FROM AROUND THE WORLD
Read a fact about me and match me to my name.

A. Goliath frog   B. Pinocchio frog   C. Tomato frog   D. Glass frog

1. You don't have to dissect me to see my insides. I have SEE-THROUGH skin. Who am I?

2. I'm as red as ketchup, but don't put me on your burger! Who am I?

3. Hello, Kitty! I'm as big as a cat. I can eat a bat! Who am I?

NO LIE!

4. I cannot tell a lie. I have a hooked nose like a beak. Nobody knew about me until 2010 – no lie! Who am I?

Answers on page 158

Stink had a Peter Parker of a secret. Not even the evil Dr Octopus could drag it out of him. Aw, who was he kidding? He couldn't hold it in one more second. He ran to the phone to call Sophie and Webster and told them to come over right away.

When they got to the house, Stink motioned for his friends to come upstairs.

"Psst!" Stink whispered. "Up here."

"Why are we whispering?" Sophie asked.

"Because. It's a secret."

He pulled out the fishbowl from under his desk. "First, I have to ask – would you guys still be my friends even if I were a frog?"

"I'd still be your friend," Sophie told him. "I'd put you in a shoe box and feed you flies."

118

"I'd still be your friend," said
Webster. "I'd carry you
in my pocket and
let you take a
bath in the sink."

"Thanks! Now,
get ready for your
eyes to pop out."

Webster gulped. Sophie
pushed her glasses up on her nose.

"Ready?" Stink asked.

"Ready," said Sophie and Webster.

"Are you sure?"

"Stink!" said Webster impatiently.

119

"I'm just saying. It's not for the faint of heart, as Peter Parker would say."

Sophie held her breath. Webster held his breath.

"Ta-da!" Stink pulled off the Spider-Man pyjama top in one swoop.

Webster stuttered. "H-h-h-he ... it's ... f-f-frog ... n-n-not..."

"Bl-bl-blue!" shouted Sophie, pointing. "Frog!"

Webster's eyes were as round as quarters. "Smurf city!"

"Meet King Otto the Third! Radioactive mutant ninja frog!" said Stink.

"So, you mean, he glows blue because he's *radioactive*?" asked Sophie.

Stink nodded. He told them all about finding the freaky frog. He showed them the spot on his arm that he would never ever wash.

Stink told them about his new-found frog tendencies. He stuck out his tongue and touched the tip of his nose to prove it.

"Look!" Sophie pointed to Stink's feet. "Your toes. They're part webbed!"

"You're turning into a frog from the feet up," said Webster.

"Just my second and third toes," said
Stink. "I got it from my Grandma Lou.
She has the same thing. Judy, too."

"Phew," said Webster.

"But..." Stink wiggled his toes. "Now that you mention it, it *does* look a bit more webbed than normal."

"And how else do you explain the raisins, and the worms and swimming in the sink and—"

"And you have a best friend named *Web*-ster," said Webster.

"And your favourite colour is *green*," said Sophie. "Yipes! We have to do something. Before you start *glowing*."

"We'd better talk to Jasper," said Stink. "Stat."

"Huh?" said Webster.

"Huh?" said Sophie.

"That means pronto, super-quick, right away!"

"Do you think your mum or dad will take us?" asked Webster.

"Let's ask," said Sophie.

"Tally ho!" said Stink, just like Peter Parker.

✳ ✳ ✳

Stink told Mum he had an A-1 super-important frog mission. Mum dropped Stink and his friends off at the Nature Centre.

Jasper O'Farrell told Stink he'd seen his share of frogs. He'd seen two-toed and three-legged frogs. He'd seen frogs with extra legs and frogs with extra eyes and frogs with no legs and frogs with only one eye. He'd seen frogs with shrunken heads and frogs with kinked tails. He'd even seen albino frogs.

But never-ever-ever in his long-legged life had Jasper O'Farrell seen a true blue frog up close and personal.

He squinted at the blue frog from every angle. He scratched his little beard. He peered at the frog with a magnifying glass.

"Well?" Stink rocked back and forth on his feet.

Jasper scratched his tiny beard some more.

"What do you think?" asked Stink. "Is he a mutant? Is he radioactive?"

"If the frog is radioactive, and the frog licked Stink, is Stink going to start glowing in the dark?" asked Sophie.

"Are we going to have to start calling Stink *Smurf*?" asked Webster.

"I have to say, I've never seen anything like it," said Jasper.

"Freak of nature!" said Webster.

"Maybe he's a rare blue poison dart frog," said Stink. "Who hopped all the way here from South America."

"Nope. I don't think so. I don't want to leap to conclusions, but—"

"*Leap* to conclusions. I get it!" said Stink.

"I'm almost sure this guy's a mutant. My professor taught me about abnormal colours in frogs. I bet this froggy's colour got messed up. He's probably missing his yellow."

"Huh?" asked Stink.

"OK. Think of art class," said Jasper. "If you mix blue and yellow paint, it looks green, right?" All three kids nodded. "It's the same for a frog. They have three kinds of pigment cells, and the top one is yellow. If they're missing the yellow, they look blue to us."

"Cosmic," said Stink.

"Thanks for bringing him in, Stink. This is better than a barking tree frog! I'd like to show him to my professor. Then we'll see if we can release this little guy safely back into the wild."

"Sure," said Stink. He looked at the Frog Logs all over Jasper's desk. "Hey, did we count a lot of frogs last night?"

"We sure did," said Jasper. "More than I thought. That's the good news.

The bad news is that there are three kinds of chorus frogs, and we only heard two kinds."

"Bummer," said Stink. "Should we count again?"

"We were going to wait till next year," said Jasper. "But now we might well have another frog count this summer."

"Sweet," said Stink. "That's only 80-something days away."

Jasper laughed.

"Plus," said Stink, "it gives me time to knock on doors and get the neighbours to stop using fertilizers and stuff that's messing up the frogs."

"Good thinking," said Jasper, tapping the side of his head.

"We'll help you, Stink," said Sophie.

"Yeah, we want to save the frogs too," said Webster.

Jasper walked Stink and his friends to the door. "Bye, King Otto the Third," Stink and his friends called.

"Be careful he doesn't lick you," Sophie warned Jasper.

"Yeah," said Stink. "You might suddenly start eating raisins or get the urge to make mud pies or sleep in the basement or go swimming in the sink."

Jasper raised one eyebrow at Stink.

"I'm just saying."

Stink turned to leave. "Bye, Jasper. If you start to glow in the dark, call me."

The next day, when Sophie and Webster came over, Stink was sitting on his bed, wearing his swimming goggles.

"What's he doing?" asked Webster.

"I don't know," said Judy. "He hasn't moved his head for an hour. And he wants me to call him Frog Eyes."

"Frogs don't move their heads," said Stink. "Just their eyes."

"Why are you wearing goggles inside the house?" Sophie asked.

135

"No swimming today," said Webster. "It's Sunday."

"It's my third eyelid," said Stink. "Frogs have an extra eyelid so they can see underwater."

Judy snorted. "He still thinks he's turning into a frog. No lie."

Webster shined a flashlight in Stink's eyes. "He is blinking a lot. Frogs blink a lot too."

Sophie touched his arm. "His skin does feel a little cool. And slippery."

"But whoever heard of a frog that doesn't swim?" said Judy. "You won't even put your head underwater, Stink.

Face it. Once a Polliwog, always a Polliwog."

"For your information," said Stink, "a polliwog is a tadpole. And a tadpole turns into a frog."

Judy shrugged.

"And I'm blinking because that's what frogs do," said Stink. "Frogs use their eyeballs to swallow bugs. No lie. They don't have teeth, so their eyes push back in their head to force the food down."

Webster looked at Sophie. Sophie looked at Webster.

"But you don't eat with your eye-balls," said Webster.

"And you definitely don't eat bugs," said Sophie.

Stink got up. He air-swam over to his desk. He fished inside his desk drawer till he found something. Something better than an Almost Joy candy bar. Better than a box of Milk Dudes. Better than a jawbreaker!

A lollipop. Not just any old lollipop. A real-live dead-bug lollipop! A bright orange, sugar-free lollipop with a for-real cricket inside.

Blink. Blink-blink.

"You're not really going to lick that, are you?" asked Webster.

Blink-blink-blink.

"Please tell me you're not going to eat a cricket," Sophie said.

"Where'd you get that thing?" Judy asked.

"Had it. Since last Halloween. I just never wanted to eat it before." Stink took off the wrapper and stuck out his tongue.

L-i-i-i-i-ck!

Stink slurped his sucker. He licked that lollipop with his long tongue. He got sticky stuff on his nose and he licked that too.

When he got to the cricket inside, he took a bite. *Munch-munch!* He took another bite. *CRUNCH!*

He swallowed. *Blinkblinkblinkblink-blink. GULP!*

Stink smiled, showing off a tiny cricket leg stuck in his teeth!

"Ick!" squealed Judy, making a face.

"Bluck!" said Sophie, sticking out her tongue.

"Grosssss!" squealed Webster, holding his tummy.

From behind his goggles, Stink's eyes bugged out of his head. He looked a little green. He clutched his stomach.

"Are you going to be sick?" Judy asked.

"*I'm* going to be sick!" said Webster.

"He looks like he's going to croak," said Sophie.

Stink burped. He pushed back his goggles. "Crickets taste like ... popcorn!" He grinned ear to ear, smiling wider than a Pacman frog.

* * *

On Monday, Stink had frogs on the brain all through Social Studies and Maths and Art. He had frogs on the brain through lunch and breaktime. He had frogs on the brain till the bell rang.

At last it was time for after-school swimming!

In the car on the way to swimming, Stink tested his frog ability. He stuck out his long tongue and – *slurp!* – touched the tip of his nose.

"Still got it," said Stink.

On his way to the pool, Stink

leapfrogged over Sophie in the grass. He leapfrogged over Webster. He even leapfrogged over Sophie *and* Webster.

At the pool, Stink put on his swimming trunks. Stink put on his flippers. Stink put on his goggles. He hopped into the pool without sticking a single toe in first.

"Good for you, Stink!" Cammy called out. She was helping another Polliwog to float.

Stink practised holding his breath. Stink splashed a little water on his face. He blew bubbles with his mouth.

He blew bubbles with his nose. He blew bubbles with his nose and mouth at the same time!

With his head above water, Stink floated on a pool noodle, like a frog on a lily pad.

Cammy swam over to him. "Okay, let's see what you got, Stink Moody."

Stink looked at the spot on his arm where he'd been licked by a mutant ninja frog. He pictured King Otto the Third in his mind's eye. He called on his newfound frog power.

And then, it happened.

Stink took in a big breath. Stink puffed out his cheeks. Stink squeezed his eyes shut and thought froggy thoughts.

I am the frog. I own the night. I am one with the water.

In the blink of a frog's eye, Stink put his face in the water. He held one-two-three fingers in the air. Stink held his breath, underwater, for three whole seconds! He even opened his eyes.

"Stink! You did it! Good for you," said Cammy. "Eiffel Tower!" Cammy held her hands in the air and they double high-fived.

"Stink Frog lives!" shouted Stink, pumping his fist in the air and smiling like a superhero.

"Let's see you cross the shallow end, Stink. Without your pool noodle this time."

Stink froggy-kicked his way across the shallow end, dunking his face in the water and coming up for air. The lane marker stretched across the pool, wiggling like a giant worm. Reflections shimmered in the water like silvery coins. Shadows of pool flags waved at Stink when he reached the other end.

"Wow. I've never seen you swim like that," said Cammy. "You must be part frog or something."

"Just call me Stink Frog," said Stink. "It's my gift and my curse."

"Your what?"

"Nothing. Never mind. Just something Peter Parker said."

"So, do you want to play a game of London Bridge today?"

"Nope."

"O-K. How about Poison? Pop Goes the Weasel? Beware the Dogfish?"

"But you don't even have to put your head under water for those games.

Those games are for Polliwogs."

Cammy looked out over all her Polliwogs splashing in the shallow end. "You know what, Stink? I like to think there just might be a little frog in each of us."

Stink nodded.

"What do you say we show these Polliwogs how it's done? How about if I toss a quarter in the shallow end and you dive for it?"

"Can I hold my nose?" Stink asked.

"Sure."

"And wear my goggles?"

"Of course."

"Do I get to keep the quarter?" Stink asked.

"Well, this *is* a big day for you. Maybe just this once." Cammy tossed the quarter and Stink dove for it. Once. Twice.

"Hey guys," Stink called out to Webster and Sophie, Judy and Riley Rottenberger. "Check me out!"

With everybody watching, Cammy tossed the quarter again. Stink dove underwater. In no time, he popped up, sputtering and spluttering, but he was holding the shiny coin.

Stink's friends clapped. His sister cheered. Other Sharks and Dolphins and Polliwogs cheered too.

Wait just a Millard Fillmore minute! This quarter was a dollar! A shiny Millard Fillmore presidential one-dollar coin!

"Ribbet!" said Stink.

Goodbye, Polliwog. Hello, Frog!

Creature Feature Answer Key

Creature Feature #1: Fun Frogs of Virginia

1. C, Bullfrog
2. D, Chorus frog
3. A, Pickerel frog
4. B, Northern cricket frog

Creature Feature #2: More Fun Frogs of Virginia

1. C, Northern spring peeper frog
2. B, Northern green frog
3. D, Wood frog
4. A, Southern leopard frog

Creature Feature #3: Freaky Frogs From Around the World

1. D, Glass frog
2. C, Tomato frog
3. A, Goliath frog
4. B, Pinocchio frog

Stink Moody has his own website!

(One he doesn't have to share with his bossy older sister, Judy)

for the latest in all things Stink, visit

www.stinkmoody.com

where you can:

- Test your Stink knowledge with an I.Q. quiz

- Write and illustrate your own comic strip

- Create your own guinea pig: choose its colours, name it and e-mail it to a friend!

- Guess Stink's middle name

- Learn way-not-boring stuff about Megan McDonald and Peter H. Reynolds

- Read the Stink-y fact of the week!